Hello!

When I was a kid in northern New York, Halloween meant making a costume that could fit over a heavy jacket, because there was always the chance we'd be trick-or-treating in the snow. I loved walking down the street, the wind rattling the last leaves on the trees, and ghosts and goblins hiding behind the bushes. It was a good kind of spooky.

Halloween can be a dangerous time for pets, though. Before you go out, make sure they're safe inside your home. Some people think Halloween is a time to play tricks on animals. That's cruel. If you see someone doing that, tell your parents or another adult right away.

Don't forget about giving your pet a Halloween treat, either. Look up safe recipes or decorate their cages for the season. I don't know about your animals, but mine love ghost stories.

Boo!

Laurie Halse Anderson

Edmond, I'll miss your great smile! Mrs. Jerome 2015

Collect All the Vet Volunteers Books

LAURIE HALSE ANDERSON

Masks

PUFFIN BOOKS
An Imprint of Penguin Group (USA) Inc.

ACKNOWLEDGMENTS

Thanks to Kim Michels, D.V.M.

PUFFIN BOOKS
Published by the Penguin Group
Penguin Young Readers Group, 345 Hudson Street, New York, New York 10014, U.S.A.
Penguin Group (Canada), 90 Eglinton Avenue East, Suite 700, Toronto, Ontario, Canada M4P 2Y3
(a division of Pearson Penguin Canada Inc.)
Penguin Books Ltd, 80 Strand, London WC2R 0RL, England
Penguin Ireland, 25 St Stephen's Green, Dublin 2, Ireland (a division of Penguin Books Ltd)
Penguin Group (Australia), 250 Camberwell Road, Camberwell, Victoria 3124, Australia
(a division of Pearson Australia Group Pty Ltd)
Penguin Books India Pvt Ltd, 11 Community Centre, Panchsheel Park, New Delhi - 110 017, India
Penguin Group (NZ), 67 Apollo Drive, Rosedale, Auckland 0632, New Zealand
(a division of Pearson New Zealand Ltd)
Penguin Books (South Africa) (Pty) Ltd, 24 Sturdee Avenue,
Rosebank, Johannesburg 2196, South Africa

Registered Offices: Penguin Books Ltd, 80 Strand, London WC2R 0RL, England

First published in the United States of America by Pleasant Company Publications, 2002
Published by Puffin Books, a division of Penguin Young Readers Group, 2007, 2012

1 3 5 7 9 10 8 6 4 2

Copyright © Laurie Halse Anderson 2002, 2012
Title page photo © 2011, Bob Krasner

LIBRARY OF CONGRESS CATALOGING-IN-PUBLICATION DATA
Anderson, Laurie Halse.
Masks / Laurie Halse Anderson.
p. cm.
Summary: After assisting with her own cat's emergency surgery,
Sunita decides she can no longer work with animals and accepts an internship at a lab,
unaware that the research conducted there includes animal testing.
ISBN 978-0-14-241257-2
[1. Animals—Treatment—Fiction. 2. Animal experimentation—Fiction.
3. Cats—Fiction. 4. Veterinarians—Fiction.] I. Title.
PZ7.A54385Mas 2009 [Fic]—dc22
2009008763

Printed in the United States of America

To Suzanne Weyn, with thanks

Masks

Chapter One

. . . .

You'll make an awesome tiger, Sunita," Maggie tells me as we spread our art materials across her kitchen table. It's Thursday afternoon, a week before Halloween. We've decided we'd better start making costumes for the big Halloween party at the Ambler Town Center.

"Your dark eyes will look so cool through the mask," Maggie adds.

She's totally focusing on my costume now. Once Maggie sets her mind to a project, she locks in. Sometimes she reminds me of a bulldog—playful and fun, but once she sinks her teeth into something, it's awfully hard to shake her loose!

She studies me intently, working out my costume in her mind. "I've never seen a tiger with long black hair, though. Maybe we can make you an orange-striped hood to wear. Or a scarf out of tiger-striped fabric." She smiles. "Being a tiger is just perfect for you."

I'm surprised and pleased that Maggie sees me that way, but I'm not sure that being a tiger fits my personality. I think of tigers as fierce and strong. I'm more on the shy, timid side.

Being a tiger does fit with my number-one passion in life: cats. There are lots of other things I like—computers and computer games, ballet, reading (especially about animals), and collecting Ganesha statues. (Ganesha's a sweet Hindu god with a boy's body and an elephant's head.) But there's nothing I love more than cats— domestic cats, wild cats, large and small cats.

Another reason being a tiger fits me is that one home of the tiger is India, and that's where my ancestors came from. Both my mother and father are doctors who have lived in this country for many years, but we stay in touch with our Indian background.

There's a knock on the kitchen door, and Maggie opens it. David Hutchinson and Brenna

Lake come in. Brenna has a shopping bag stuffed with even more art supplies. She begins adding them to the pile of materials we've already loaded onto the table.

"Are you going to be a horse for Halloween?" I ask David. He's wild about horses.

He shakes his head. "A vampire. I vant to suck your blood!"

"He can't figure out how to make a horse mask," Brenna adds.

"I could too!" David objects. "I just think being a horse would be sort of geeky."

"Mucho geeky," Maggie agrees.

"What will you be?" I ask her.

"A vet, of course," Maggie replies.

"You don't need a mask for that," Brenna says.

"Yes, you do—a surgical mask. Gran has a ton of them in the supply cabinet," Maggie says.

"That's too easy. No fair," Brenna says. "I want to be something unusual—maybe a unicorn. Is that too babyish? I don't know. I still have to think about it."

Dr. Mac comes in and runs her hand through her short white hair as she surveys all our stuff—colored paper, yarn, glue, markers, beads and buttons, paints, pipe cleaners, and stickers. "Wow!" she says. "What's the big project?"

Dr. Mac is Dr. J.J. MacKenzie, veterinarian extraordinaire. She lives in a big brick house with Maggie. Although Dr. Mac is Maggie's grandmother, she's so full of energy that she doesn't seem like a regular grandmother to me.

Dr. Mac and Maggie live with lots of animals. Besides their cat, Socrates, and their dog, Sherlock Holmes, they have a house full of animal patients. That's because Dr. Mac runs Dr. Mac's Place Veterinary Clinic right here, attached to her own house. She treats any animals that come through the door—pets, strays, and even wild animals. People who bring in strays or wild animals pay her what they can or sometimes nothing at all.

I volunteer at Dr. Mac's Place, along with Maggie, David, and Brenna. I love working at the clinic. In fact, my dream is to be a vet someday.

"We're making masks for the Halloween party at Town Center," Maggie tells Dr. Mac. "Do you need us, Gran?"

Dr. Mac shakes her head. "So far it's been a slow morning. If something comes up, I'll holler," she says as she leaves the kitchen.

"Guess who I saw this morning?" Brenna asks as she redoes the elastic at the end of her long brown braid. She continues without waiting for an answer. "As I was coming here, I saw the woman who just moved into that big old converted barn down the road."

"Does she have any kids?" David asks.

Brenna shrugs her slim shoulders. "I didn't see any," she answers. "My mom heard that she's some kind of artist."

"That barn would be great for a studio," I say. "It's so big, and the last owners put in skylights."

"I saw the woman at the market," Maggie says, brushing her red hair out of her eyes. "She was wearing all black, and she has wild gray hair that makes her look like a witch!"

"Oh, my gosh!" Brenna cries. "Listen to this! When I saw her, she was pulling a big black kettle out of the back of her station wagon!"

"Oh, man, she's a witch for sure!" David says, his eyes lighting up.

Brenna wraps her arms around herself and shivers. "Whoa—a witch! And just in time for Halloween! Cool!"

"I can picture her with the black kettle," David

says. "Bubble, bubble, toil and trouble!" He mimics a cackling witch voice, pretending to stir an imaginary potion.

As David does his witch act, a black-and-white tuxedo cat strolls in. It's my cat, Mittens. I brought her with me this morning, because at my house repairmen are fixing our front steps, and all the hammering was scaring her. Mittens jumps up onto the table, and I scratch her between the ears. "Hi, honey," I murmur.

Before she was mine, Mittens was a stray. I first saw her one day when she came wandering around the clinic.

"Let's go check out the witch," David says. "I've never seen a real one."

"Oh, come on!" I say, laughing. "You don't really think she's a witch!"

"You never know," David says in a low, creepy voice, his eyes darting mysteriously from side to side. "At Halloween, anything is possible."

"David, you're so weird," I tease.

"I think there might really be such things as witches," Brenna says. "They can do good stuff, too."

"Yeah," Maggie agrees. "I mean, people have

believed in them for so long. Could people be totally wrong?"

"Sure they could be wrong!" I argue. "People used to think the earth was flat, and that the sun revolved around the earth, and all sorts of crazy things."

"I heard a story once," David begins in a spooky tone. "During the Salem witch trials, a woman was hanged for being a witch. But as they put the noose around her neck, she put this horrible curse on the people. She swore she would dance on their graves.

"Every year on the anniversary of her death, footprints appeared on the graves of anyone who had watched the witch get hanged. When people tried to wipe away the footprints, their hands were covered with blood."

"Ew!" Brenna cries with a shiver.

"Creepy," Maggie agrees.

I smile and roll my eyes. Spooky stuff like witches, ghosts, and ancient curses are fun at Halloween, but they're not for real. I'll take scientific explanations every time.

Mittens begins batting markers across the table. One of the markers rolls off and falls to the floor. As I bend to pick it up, Mittens starts chewing on a button. I pull it away from her. My cat has been known to eat strange things.

She pounces on my hand with her claws sheathed. "OK! OK! I get the message," I say to her. I pull a length of thick orange yarn out of its skein and cut it off. I dangle the yarn in front of Mittens. "Here you go, Mittens—catch this!"

I reach high and jiggle the yarn. Mittens rises on her back legs and swings her paws at it.

"Go on! Catch it!" I coax, pulling the yarn just out of her reach. "You can get it, Mittens." I lower the yarn just a bit so she can have the satisfaction of capturing it.

We laugh as Mittens pounces ferociously. She reminds me of a lioness, hunting out on the savanna. She snatches the whole piece of yarn out of my hand and then sits on it, protecting her prize.

"Good job!" we praise her, clapping. "Way to go!"

I stroke my cat's silky fur. I'd wanted a cat for so long before my mother finally gave in. At first, she had a million excuses—cats shed, cats tear up the furniture, and so on. When she finally let me have Mittens, it was the happiest day of my life.

I named my cat Mittens because she looks like she's wearing two little white mittens on her front paws.

I've never met a more affectionate cat. She's always nuzzling me and giving me scratchy little love-kiss licks. I return those with a kiss on her furry forehead.

David cuts a piece of white cardboard into the shape of a face. He cuts out the eyeholes, then a slit for the mouth. "Should I draw the fangs or make them with clay?" he wonders aloud.

Suddenly there's a loud bang from outside, as if something heavy has just fallen. Some animal makes a screechy, screaming sound. The howl becomes more high-pitched.

"That is definitely a cat!" I say—a very upset, angry, threatening cat.

We jump up and rush to the door. It sounds like a cat fight, but I can hear only one cat screaming. I get to the door first and pull it open, but before I can step out, Maggie grabs my shoulder, holding me back. "Look out!" she cries as a black blur streaks by my feet.

Chapter Two

. . . .

What was that?" I gasp.

Behind me, David shouts. "There it is! It's a cat, a black cat!"

I see it for just a second as it races off into some bushes.

"Sunita, a black cat just passed right in front of you. You know what that means!" David says.

"Bad luck," Maggie finishes solemnly. She says it so seriously, I think she might actually believe it.

"Oh, yeah, sure," I laugh. "Like I really believe that."

We step out into the yard. Immediately, I see what fell over—a garbage can. And, just as immediately, I smell a very familiar odor. We all smell it.

"Skunk!" we shout all together.

Right on cue, a fat skunk waddles out of the overturned garbage can.

"Oh, how cute!" Maggie says.

It is cute. Smelly, but cute. Obviously it sprayed the area because something upset it—either the garbage can turning over or a confrontation with the cat.

Poor cat. I hope its owner will know it needs a bath in tomato juice to help get rid of the smell.

Brenna squeezes her nose shut. "P.U.!" she says in a pinched, nasal voice. "What was the skunk doing in the garbage can, anyway?"

"Skunks sleep in the daytime," Maggie says. "Maybe it fell in there during the night while it was looking for food."

"That's possible," Brenna agrees. "Maybe it got stuck in there and then fell asleep once the sun came up."

"And the cat woke it up," I add. Then it occurs to me: If the cat was looking for food in the garbage can, then maybe it's a stray. If it doesn't have an owner, how will it get rid of the skunk smell?

"That cat was really speeding," David says. "I bet it never expected to find a skunk in there when it started nosing around."

The skunk waddles over to a clump of trees. "Let's get out of here," Brenna suggests, pinching her nose shut once again.

"Have you guys ever seen that cat around here before?" I ask as we return to the kitchen.

"I've never seen it before," Maggie says.

"Well, if it ever comes around again, we'll be able to smell it coming," David jokes.

"I wonder—" Maggie begins, then pauses.

"What?" I prod her. It drives me crazy when people don't complete a thought.

"Doesn't it seem strange that a woman who looks like a witch moves in nearby, and suddenly a black cat shows up?" Maggie asks.

"A witch and her mysterious black cat," David says ominously.

"You guys!" I say with a laugh. Seems like the Halloween bug has bitten them hard.

"Believe what you like," Maggie says. She

picks up a pair of scissors and begins cutting into a piece of construction paper, as if she's made up her mind on the subject.

Is it really possible she does believe that a witch—complete with cauldron and black cat—has actually moved in down the road?

"I want to meet her," Maggie says. "I'll be able to tell just by looking at her."

David laughs. "How? Do you think she'll be wearing a black cloak and a pointed hat?"

"I'll know by looking at her eyes," Maggie says confidently. "I can tell things about people from their eyes."

"You should get out your telescope, Maggie," I say. "Then you can look out the window and watch her zoom past the moon tonight."

Maggie rolls her eyes at me. "Oh, very funny!"

Mittens is still sitting contentedly on the table. "All the excitement's over, sweet girl," I say. I look at my watch. "Uh-oh, time for you and me to get home for dinner." I scoop up Mittens. "See you on Saturday, guys." Friday's my afternoon to watch Horabil and Jessica, my five year old twin brother and sister.

"Watch out for witches!" David cackles as we head out the door.

Oh, brother.

• • • • •

I wake up late on Saturday morning. I reach over to pet Mittens, who always sleeps next to my pillow, but she's not there.

"Mittens, sweetie, where are you?" I call.

There's no answer. That's odd—Mittens always wants to be fed early in the morning, and I'm the only one who feeds her. I'm used to waking up to her purring in my ear and kneading her paws on my shoulder. I get up, get dressed, and start searching. Where could she be?

Then I hear it, a faint *meow* coming from the back of my closet. I turn on the closet light and find Mittens in the back corner. She's curled up in a tight ball, and I see several places where she has vomited. Her sides are heaving in and out as if she's trying to vomit again, but it looks as if she can't. She doesn't even try to come to me.

"Mom!" I cry. But there's no answer. Mom must have already left for the hospital. And Daddy takes Harshil and Jasmine to the library on Saturday mornings.

I scoop up Mittens, wrap her in a towel, and put her in the basket on the front of my bike. It has a lid that I close and fasten. "Hang on, sweetie. I'll get you to Dr. Mac's in no time."

Chapter Three

• • • • • • • • • • •

Dr. Mac is searching for something in the supply closet. When she hears me racing into the clinic, she turns quickly. "What's wrong, Sunita?"

"It's Mittens. She's been vomiting, and she won't even move." My voice is shaking.

"Come on," she says, heading straight into the Herriot Room. I follow her with Mittens.

When I unwrap my cat, she's still curled into a tight ball. Dr. Mac carefully feels her all over. When she lightly presses my cat's belly, Mittens lets out a loud moan and hisses.

"I'm going to X-ray her," Dr. Mac tells me. "But first, I'm going to give her a sedative. She's too upset to let us get a good picture of her insides."

"What's wrong with her, Dr. Mac?" I ask.

"I hope the X-ray will tell us," she says.

I pick up Mittens and follow Dr. Mac into the X-ray room. She hands me a lead apron, gloves, and collar for protection against the harmful rays of the machine.

"First, put the lead protectors over yourself," Dr. Mac instructs. "Then lay Mittens down on her side with her legs stretched out. We'll take a second view with her lying on her back."

I do as Dr. Mac asks. The sedative has relaxed Mittens enough that she lets me lay her on her side and gently stretch her out.

Dr. Mac steps into the small room next to the X-ray machine. She hits some buttons and the machine X-rays Mittens. The whole procedure takes only a few moments.

I remove my shields and return with Mittens to the Herriot Room while Dr. Mac develops the film. Brenna, David, and Maggie have come in to wait with me. "She'll be OK, Sunita," Brenna says "You know Dr. Mac won't let anything bad happen to Mittens."

I nod, knowing Mittens will get the best

possible care. But I'm not as confident that nothing will go wrong. I've worked at the clinic long enough to know that animal injuries can be unpredictable.

After a few minutes, Dr. Mac comes in to show us the X-rays. She places them on the lighted view box. "Everything looks fine except the intestines. They're all bunched up, making what we call a 'string sign' on the X-ray. Could Mittens have eaten some string in the last few days?"

"Yarn!" Tears spring to my eyes. "She must have eaten the yarn from my tiger mask! Is that what's hurting her?" I ask.

"Not exactly. Sometimes yarn can pass through a cat's system without any pain or damage. In this case, the intestines are trying to move the yarn through Mittens' system, but the yarn has gotten stuck. The pulling has caused her intestines to bunch up, and that's why she's in pain and vomiting. We're going to have to operate right away, Sunita."

I feel so horribly, terribly guilty. I know cats shouldn't be left alone with string or yarn. I know it! When that stray cat tipped over the garbage, I let myself be distracted and forgot all about Mittens. Even though I try to hold back, my lower lip quivers and a tear rolls down my cheek. It seems so babyish to cry in the middle of an emergency. Maggie puts her hand on my shoulder.

Dr. Mac turns to me. "I know it's scary, Sunita, but try to stay calm."

I can hardly believe what's happening. I wish I could just wake up and discover this is all a bad nightmare. How could I have let this happen to an animal who trusts me so completely, who relies on me to take care of her?

Dr. Mac pats my shoulder. "Don't blame yourself. These things just happen sometimes."

Yes. They happen to careless, unthinking people who shouldn't be allowed around animals.

I feel a tingling in my nose and under my eyes, which is a warning that I'm about to cry. I turn away to get myself under control. When the tingling stops, I look back at my friends. The three of them wear serious, concerned expressions. Maggie forces a tight smile meant to be comforting.

"I want to help with the operation," I say.

"Are you sure, Sunita? You don't have to," Dr. Mac says.

"I'm sure." I have to be there for Mittens. She depends on me, and I've already let her down once. I don't want to do it twice. I go and change into scrubs.

When I step into the surgery room and see Mittens stretched out limply on the surgery table, I take in a quick, sharp breath. My hands shake and I hold them together tightly to stop the quivering. Mittens looks ... dead. The room starts spinning. I stagger and grip the edge of a stool.

Dr. Mac looks up. "Steady," she says. "She's only anesthetized. Sit and put your head down."

I do as she suggests. After a minute, the room stops spinning. When I look up, Mittens' belly is shaved and Dr. Mac is swabbing it with orange iodine.

"Maybe you should let Maggie and me handle this," Dr. Mac suggests as Maggie comes in.

"I'm OK," I say. "I want to help."

Dr. Mac nods.

I set the surgical instruments out on a tray, as I've done so many times before. Dr. Mac inserts an I.V. into Mittens' foreleg. "She'll need fluids during surgery," Dr. Mac says, "and we'll start her on high levels of antibiotics, too."

Maggie monitors the anesthetic as well as Mittens' vital signs. Then Dr. Mac reaches out to me with her right hand. "Scalpel."

I place the instrument firmly in her out-
stretched hand the way she's taught us. At least I
try, but my hand shakes slightly. Dr. Mac notices
and looks at me sharply, with concerned eyes.
For a moment I think she'll tell me to leave, but
she turns back to Mittens.

Maggie adjusts a small, intense lamp on
Mittens as Dr. Mac makes a precise slit up my
cat's belly. I've seen her do this on other animals
before, but this time I have to turn away.

I try not to look at Mittens, but sometimes I
just have to peek. Dr. Mac makes small cuts along
the intestine with the scalpel, then tugs out the
yarn a little at a time. The process of snipping the
intestine and pulling out the yarn takes forty-five
minutes. It takes her another half hour to stitch
Mittens' intestines and belly back up. Finally Dr.
Mac flushes out Mittens' abdomen with saline
before closing.

"Done," she announces. On a white towel
beside Mittens are inch-long pieces of orange
yarn. "I've removed all the yarn, but I'm afraid
she's not out of the woods yet, Sunita," Dr. Mac
tells me.

"What could go wrong?" I ask.

"Mittens had a small tear in her intestines.

That happens sometimes as the yarn pulls—it causes the intestines to rupture. When bacteria from the intestines leak out into the abdomen, we have to be concerned about an infection called peritonitis," she tells me. "All we can do now is wait and watch."

When I saw all that yarn laying there beside Mittens, I'd thought the danger had passed. Now I'm scared all over again. "This peritonitis," I say. "Is it ... I mean, could it ..."

"In a severe case it could be fatal." Dr. Mac answers my unasked question.

I blink back tears.

Dr. Mac turns to me. "Sunita, try not to worry. Everything probably will be fine. I just have to be honest with you about the possibilities."

"I know," I say.

"Mittens will sleep for a few hours now," Dr. Mac explains. "You can leave if you need to."

"Thanks," I say as I change out of my scrubs, "but I want to be here when Mittens wakes up."

David and Brenna are still there when Maggie and I walk out into the waiting room. "Mittens came through surgery OK, but there's danger of infection," I tell them. "There's nothing more to do for her right now, but I'm going to stay here until she wakes up."

"We'll wait with you, then," says David.

We try to go back to our mask making, but none of us has the heart for it anymore. After a while I go to the front desk and start putting all the loose papers in order and filing them away. Brenna and David clean the kennels, and Maggie tackles the supply closet.

After what seems like forever, Dr. Mac tells me that Mittens is starting to wake up. "She came through surgery well, Sunita," Dr. Mac says.

I walk back to the recovery room and enter quietly, so that I won't startle Mittens. She's lying on her side, and she's looking at me with dull, glazed eyes. She's still groggy from the anesthetic. She opens her mouth to meow, but no sound comes out. I open her cage and stroke gently behind her ears, in her favorite spot.

"I'm so sorry, sweetie." Tears roll down my cheek. "The last thing in the world I wanted to do was hurt you. Dr. Mac's going to take great care of you, and I'll come here to visit you every day."

I kiss her furry forehead, and she starts to purr softly. "You get some rest now. That's what you need most to get better," I say as I close the cage door.

When I come back out into the waiting room, my friends all look at me anxiously. "Mittens is awake and OK so far. I'm going to go home."

"Are you all right?" Brenna asks. "Do you want us to come with you?"

"No, but thanks," I reply. "I'll be OK."

I bike down the road, pedaling slowly as I ride by the renovated barn the new woman in town has moved into. I remember an article I once read on witches. It claimed that witches were simply women who knew a lot about folk cures for sickness. They worked mostly with plants and herbs, using cures that had been handed down from woman to woman through time. Some people, especially men, feared these women because they didn't understand what they did.

Wouldn't it be nice if I could stop off at this woman's house and ask her for something that would heal Mittens? I stop my bike and gaze at the barn-house, wishing for some kind of magic.

The sun reflects off an upper window, and I see something move. I have the uneasy feeling that someone is looking at me.

I get back on the bike seat and begin pedaling again—a bit faster than before.

Chapter Four

● ● ● ● ● ● ● ● ● ● ●

"Sunita's home!" shouts Harshil when I walk in the door.

Jasmine races down the stairs. "Sunita, will you play Barbies with me?"

Playing Barbies is just about the last thing I feel like doing right now. "Later, OK?" I beg off.

"Would you read me these books I got from the library?" Harshil asks, holding up three picture books.

"I'll do that later, too," I promise. "Why don't you two watch TV?"

Jasmine makes a disappointed face. "We've been watching TV all afternoon."

I know my mother is at the hospital on Saturday afternoons, so I don't even bother to hunt for her. My father is probably buried in his study as usual.

Out of habit, I head for the kitchen, but I realize I'm not hungry at all. I pull open the refrigerator, stare into it, then shut it again without taking anything out. When I turn, I see my father at the table, cutting a piece of cake for himself.

He looks at me and frowns thoughtfully. "Why so glum?" he asks.

I sit in a kitchen chair and tell him all about what happened to Mittens. He forgets about his cake and nods as he listens.

"I feel so terrible," I say at the end of my story. "Maybe I'm not responsible enough to take care of animals."

He folds his arms and sits back in his chair, studying me. Is he disappointed in me? I hope he doesn't say it was not my fault, because I know better than that. If it wasn't my fault, whose was it?

"Try not to worry too much," he says. "Dr. MacKenzie is very capable. But Sunita, perhaps it's time for a change."

His remark takes me by surprise. "What kind of change?"

"Well," he begins, "perhaps it is time to try something new. The other day, an associate asked me if you would be interested in an internship at his research lab. I didn't even present it to you because I know you're busy with your work at the clinic. But maybe now you would like to give this lab work a try."

If I take this job, I'll have less time to volunteer at Dr. Mac's Place. But maybe that would be a good thing.

"What kind of work do they do at the lab?" I ask.

My father smiles. "It's a veterinary lab. They create new medicines for animals."

"That does sound pretty interesting," I say. It would be a way to help animals without putting them in danger by my carelessness.

"What do you think?" my father prods.

"I'll give it a try," I say. Why not?

My father smiles as he gets up from his chair. "I'll call my friend, Dr. Dan Green, and tell him you're interested. Don't go away. I'll be right back."

After a few minutes, my father hurries back in, looking excited. "The internship spot is still available. You can start on Tuesday. I think you'll love it," he says enthusiastically. "I spent a summer working in a research lab and found it fascinating."

I guess he hopes it will be the same with me.

No sooner does my father return to his study than Jasmine runs into the kitchen. "You're just sitting here. Now can you play Barbies?"

"Later," I remind her.

"This is later! Besides, you're not doing anything," Jasmine insists.

Harshil comes in, holding his library books. "Is it later yet?" he asks.

"Later is when Sunita is playing Barbies with me," Jasmine tells him.

"No way," Harshil replies. "Later is when she reads my books to me."

Listening to them bicker is about to drive me insane. Without a word, I slip out the kitchen door that leads to our backyard. They're so busy fighting, they don't even see me leave.

Something black slinks under one of the lawn chairs at the back of the yard. Squinting into the late afternoon sun, I see that it's a cat.

I walk slowly, casually, toward the lawn chair. The cat will bolt if I approach too quickly. It could be the black cat we saw in Dr. Mac's yard

30

the other day. When I'm about three feet away, I sniff. Skunk. It's the same cat, all right.

Huge green eyes stare at me. The cat seems torn between wanting to run away and wanting to be friendly. I move a little closer.

This is one amazing-looking cat. It has no tail and has huge paws. Maybe it has six toes. A breed called the Cymric has no tail and six toes. This cat also has a nip out of its left ear, probably from a fight.

The poor cat's black fur is so matted. If that matting continues and it's not able to groom itself, it may begin to scratch and its skin will get infected.

Crouching down, I look at the cat directly. In a book about cat behavior that I once read, it said that looking directly at a cat tells it that you want to be friends and mean it no harm.

The cat stares back at me. Its eyes are open wide and its ears are back, which means it's afraid. Maybe it has a good reason to be afraid. The other day I saw an article on the Internet about keeping cats safe in October. It said that some horrible people like to hurt and even kill cats around Halloween. These people range from gang members who think it's cool to torture cats to people who are seriously into dark magic. There are even people who believe that cats have evil powers and all sorts of crazy stuff like that.

It's dangerous for this black cat to be outside around Halloween. I'd sure want someone to keep Mittens inside if she somehow got lost at this time of year. My mother probably wouldn't allow me to keep a stray cat in the house, but I bet Dr. Mac would board it, at least until Halloween is over.

"Here, kitty," I call in a singsong, friendly way. "Are you hungry? Would you like to come with me? I can feed you. I can even help you out with those clumps of hair." I stretch out my hand, wishing I had some food to offer it.

The cat steps forward cautiously. "Come on, kitty, kitty," I coax. "Come to me." It stops and then takes another step. Soon it'll be within my reach.

Suddenly the kitchen door slams. Harshil and Jasmine run outside.

The cat jumps back, then bolts.

Chapter Five

· · · · · · · · · · ·

It's not easy to track a black cat in the dying light. The cat scrambles in and out of the trees' shadows. Once it stops to look back over its shoulder at me, but each time it decides to keep going. Finally I lose track of it altogether.

Disappointed, I head back toward my house. In the distance, I hear my mother call to Jasmine and Harshil, telling them to come in. If she's home from the hospital, it must be after six o'clock.

Where will the cat sleep tonight? Will it be able to catch any supper, wearing such a strong skunk odor?

I walk into the kitchen. My mother has begun cooking chicken. "There you are," she greets me, turning from the stove. "It's dark. I was starting to get worried."

"Sorry," I apologize. "I saw a stray cat in the yard and I was trying to catch it."

She laughs lightly. "Oh, you and your cats. I should have known. Are you all right? Your father told me what happened with Mittens."

"I'm OK, I suppose," I reply. "I'm worried though."

She nods and turns back to her cooking. "Dr. Mac will take good care of her," she says.

I wish I could feel reassured.

"I hear you've accepted an internship at AVM Labs," she mentions. "I'm very pleased, but surprised. Have you considered the amount of time it will take? You might have to cut down on your volunteering at Dr. Mac's Place. We don't want your grades to suffer."

I hesitate. Then I decide to tell her what's on my mind. "The truth is, Mom, I'm wondering if I'm meant to work closely with animals. I should have been more careful with Mittens. If I'd remembered not to leave her alone with the yarn, she wouldn't have swallowed it."

"It's not your fault, honey. Cats get into all sorts of things they're not supposed to," she says. "Besides, you love helping animals. Working at the lab is a way to help them, too."

The phone rings twice, and then Jasmine bursts into the kitchen waving the cordless. "It's Maggie, for you, Sunita!" She hands the phone to me.

"Thanks." I take the phone and wander toward the living room for some privacy. "Hi, Maggie," I say.

"I have the most awesome news," she launches in right away.

"About Mittens?" I ask hopefully.

"No. Sorry," she says. "I mean, nothing bad has happened. Nothing at all has happened as far as I know. Gran is still watching her. This is about something completely different."

"Oh, OK," I say, feeling let down. "What?"

"Listen to this! Brenna's mom was right—the woman who just moved in is an artist, and she's offering a mask-making workshop. Four sessions this week for just twenty dollars! I went to the market with Brenna and her mom after you left. There was a sign-up sheet right there. I called Gran and she said I could sign up. Brenna's mom agreed, too. So I signed us all up! Can you go?"

"Hang on," I say. I ask Mom for permission and she says OK, since it's only four sessions. I tell Maggie I can.

"Great!" she says. "It starts Monday at four-thirty. Think of it—we'll be able to go in her house and look around to see if she has any potions!"

Is Maggie serious? I think of the black cat and wonder if it really does belong to that woman. Being a witch's cat is better than being no one's cat.

What am I thinking? "That's ridiculous. She's not a witch!" I tell Maggie firmly.

"Yeah, yeah, yeah...whatever," Maggie says. "But it'll be fun to get into her place and look around!"

Chapter Six

. . . .

Monday morning before school I bike over to see Mittens. She was still weak yesterday when I visited. I'm worried that she's not much better by now.

"I'm concerned about that myself," Dr. Mac admits when I ask her about it. "She shouldn't still be so weak. And her temperature is running a little high."

I slip quietly into the recovery room, open the cage door, and pet Mittens until she falls asleep. Then I gently close the door and head out to class.

After school I meet up with Maggie, Brenna, and David at Dr. Mac's Place. We'd planned to walk together to our first mask-making class. "I can't go to the class," I tell them. "I have to stay here at the clinic with Mittens."

"Her condition hasn't changed, Sunita," Dr. Mac says. "Mittens will probably sleep for a while now. Why don't you go. Mittens won't even know you're here if you stay."

"You can come back later when she's awake and knows you're here," Brenna adds.

"We'll come right back and visit her after the mask class," David suggests.

I shrug. "Well, OK." I'm not really in the mood for doing anything, but I guess I have to get my mind off Mittens somehow.

I can't seem to do it, though. As I walk down the road beside my friends, I picture Mittens lying there with her insides aching, and my nose tingles, that old crying feeling. I fight it down.

We soon come near the converted barn. It's just a little way down the road from the clinic. "Look around for any sign of witchcraft," Brenna says. "I've never seen a real witch."

"And you're not going to see one now," I say dryly

"Oh, be quiet, Sunita," Maggie says. "You're spoiling the fun."

A sign on the front door says MASK MAKERS COME IN. When Brenna opens the door, it gives a long, squealing squeak straight out of a haunted-house movie. "She's not a witch, huh?" Brenna whispers.

"Having a squeaky door doesn't make you a witch!" I whisper back.

David speaks in a mysterious, scary voice. "We'll soon see about that!" He breaks into maniacal laughter.

Maggie pokes him in the back. "You're such a weirdo!"

We walk through a shadowy foyer to a very large room with an extremely high ceiling. Two big skylights let in the orange and red light of sunset. A kitchen is separated from the rest of the room by a four-foot-high divider. Its window gives a view of the woods behind the house. Two love seats sit in front of a stone fireplace that burns with a cozy fire. To the left is a wooden table with benches on either side. Five kids I recognize from school—three girls and two boys—are already seated at one end of the table.

What interests me most, though, are the masks that completely cover the wall by the table. All the masks are animal faces made of clay or papier-mâché. An orange tiger with purple stripes outlined in gold has a mysterious smile. Is he going to be friendly or bite your hand off? It's hard to tell. A lion with a lush mane of coiled golden wire bares two gleaming white ceramic fangs.

"They're awesome," Brenna says, looking at the masks.

A gray elephant mask hangs at the very top, waving his trunk out over the rest of the masks. His tusks look like stainless steel polished to a high shine.

Right at my eye level hangs a row of house-cat masks with various spots, stripes, and colorings. I admire each of them, but the last one makes me gasp. It isn't a fantasy mask at all—it's strikingly realistic. The mask is black with startling green eyes and wild black fur.

"What?" Brenna asks me.

"That last mask," I say. "It looks like the black cat we saw last week."

"How can you tell?" David asks. "We only saw the cat for a second."

"It was in my yard Saturday night," I tell

them. "I got a very close look at it. It has a nip out of its left ear, just like this mask. That's got to be the cat."

"Welcome, everyone!" A woman wearing a long purple Indian-print skirt comes into the room. She wears a red velvet vest over a flowing white shirt. She looks around at the class, but her gaze settles on me. Like the cat, she has huge green eyes. "We've met already, haven't we?" she says to me.

My mind races. I know I've never seen her before! For some reason I picture the black cat, its green eyes staring at me. "I don't think we have," I murmur.

"Hmmm, I thought we had," she says.

I now understand why my friends think this woman is a witch. She's definitely not ugly, but she has high, sharp cheekbones and a thick mane of wild, gray-streaked black hair that hangs down past her shoulders.

She smiles at the class and begins to speak. "I am Michaela Griffin, and I will be your guide through the mysterious world of mask making." Her voice is low, melodic, and a little scratchy, which I think sounds cool.

She begins passing out bundles of bendable

wire. "We're going to create the mask framework from wire. Then we'll build it in papier-mâché. I've picked these materials because it's so easy to correct any mistakes, and papier-mâché doesn't require baking or firing in a kiln. A good coat of varnish should finish it nicely."

"Can we wear these for Halloween?" David asks.

"Yes, although I wouldn't wear your mask out in the rain," she replies. "Be careful with the mask if you wear it. I encourage you to think of your mask as a work of art rather than just a means to disguise yourself. Masks can be used to hide the real self, or to reveal it," she says. "I prefer masks that reveal. They're more interesting."

I am soon totally involved in bending and shaping my wire form. But I'm only working on a face shape. I'm not sure yet what it will be.

A few days ago, I might have begun making a tiger mask like Maggie suggested. I almost could have believed what Maggie saw in me. Now, I don't feel tigerlike at all. Which animal is careless, worried, and confused? That animal would represent me best. But I can't think of one that acts that way.

"This is fun," Brenna says. She's making a

fox mask. I nod, realizing that I haven't worried about Mittens since we walked in the door.

The time goes quickly, and soon we're cleaning up. "See you all tomorrow," Michaela says.

"What did you think of the class?" Maggie asks us as we walk down the road to the clinic.

"Fun," Brenna answers.

"Yeah, cool," David agrees.

"I think Michaela's cool," I say. "She's so mysterious."

"OK, Maggie, what did her eyes tell you?" David asks in his spooky voice.

"She's nice, but sort of unusual. I need more time to figure her out," Maggie admits.

• • • • •

We go back to the clinic to visit Mittens. She lies limp in her cage, barely managing to lift her head when we come in. Her eyes are dull and lifeless.

"Poor thing," Brenna says sympathetically.

Mittens falls asleep and we all leave quietly. In the waiting room, Dr. Mac sits behind the reception desk filling out some forms.

"Mittens is about the same, Sunita," Dr. Mac

tells me. "But her fever is not responding the way it should."

I nod.

"I'm going to watch her very closely," she says. "I'll be taking her temp every hour."

"Thanks," I say.

"How was the mask-making class?" she asks us.

"Awesome!" Brenna and David say at the same time.

"I can't wait to go back to Michaela's tomorrow," Brenna adds as she and David put on their jackets to leave.

"I can't either," Maggie agrees.

When I say nothing, they all look at me. "You liked it, too, didn't you, Sunita?" Maggie asks.

"I loved it, but I...uh...I'm not sure I can make it to the mask class tomorrow," I tell them.

"Why not?" David asks.

"I took an internship at AVM Labs. It starts tomorrow."

"Are you crazy?" Brenna demands. "You can't work at AVM!"

"Why not?" I ask.

"Animal research," Brenna replies. "AVM does

tests on animals. Animals are killed just so scientists can run tests on them. Don't tell me you didn't know that!"

I hadn't thought about any of this. I knew AVM made medicines to help animals, but I didn't realize they tested on animals, too.

Dr. Mac looks up from the front desk. "Wait a minute, Brenna," she says. "Slow down. AVM is—"

"—a kill lab," Brenna interrupts. "A bad place where they kill animals."

"It's not that simple, Brenna," Dr. Mac continues.

"It's simple to me!" Brenna says angrily.

"Many new medicines are developed at AVM," Dr. Mac insists. "The company is well-respected among veterinarians. They do very important work."

"No one asks the animals how they feel about it," Brenna says.

Dr. Mac sighs, then looks at me. "Sunita, I think an internship at AVM is a great opportunity for you. But I hope you won't stop working here at the clinic. You are so wonderful with the animals."

"Thank you," I say. "I hadn't thought about all this. And I've already agreed to show up tomorrow. I think I need to take a little break from the clinic while I go see about AVM."

I pull on my jacket and head for the door.

"You're going to hate it!" Brenna calls after me.

Chapter Seven

• • • • • • • • • • • •

When I arrive at the clinic the next morning, I find Dr. Mac in the Herriot Room with Mittens on the examining table. She has a thermometer in her hand. "One hundred and four," she reads to me. A cat's normal temperature is around one hundred degrees.

I rush to Mittens and stroke her forehead. "Peritonitis?"

"That's the most likely cause," she agrees. "I've added a second antibiotic and will continue to support her with I.V. fluids. There's a good chance this treatment will be effective."

I wish she could have said it always works, but

I know that would be unrealistic. Each animal is an individual, just like each person. Animals all react differently to medication.

When I cradle Mittens in my arms, she licks my hand weakly. "It's OK, girl," I say, scratching between her ears. "You'll be all right."

The problem is—I'm not nearly as sure as I sound.

• • • • •

That afternoon, my father picks me up from school as we'd planned. He loads my bike into the back of our SUV so I won't have to come back and get it. We drive across town to the AVM laboratory. My father seems excited and happy for me. I'm just nervous.

"Daddy, Brenna told me that they actually test on animals at AVM," I say. "They don't hurt them, do they?"

"No, I don't think the animals experience pain," he says. "They work in a humane way, and for a good cause. You'll see."

At the receptionist's desk my father asks for his friend, Dr. Green, who comes out very quickly and shakes my father's hand. "Good to see you, Ravi. This must be Sunita."

My father introduces me and we head down a spotless hallway. It has gray walls and a gray carpet. Framed black-and white photos hang on the wall. We pass doors that have glass windows on the top half. Inside are white rooms with laboratory equipment. People in white coats are intent on checking charts, moving beakers, working on computers, and performing all sorts of scientific-looking activities.

I can't help but compare AVM Labs to Dr. Mac's Place. Dr. Mac's clinic is full of colorful furniture and curtains and pictures and the noise of animals. This quiet, gray place is absolutely its opposite.

Dr. Green stops in front of a door, pushes it open, and leads us in. A woman in her late twenties stands by a desk, checking a chart on a clipboard. "Julie," Dr. Green calls to her. She looks over at us and smiles. She has light reddish-blonde hair pulled back in a ponytail, green eyes, and freckles across her nose.

"This is Julie Ames," Dr. Green says as we walk over to join her. "She's a researcher here. Julie, meet Sunita Patel, your new intern."

"Welcome, Sunita," Julie greets me.

My father jumps into the conversation. "Sunita

has excellent marks in science," he tells Julie. "She will be a big help to you." That embarrasses me, and I roll my eyes.

Julie smiles at me sympathetically.

"We'll leave Sunita in your capable hands," Dr. Green tells Julie.

"Pleased to meet you," my father says to Julie, shaking her hand. He gives me a quick wave before leaving with Dr. Green.

"Ready for your first job, Sunita?" Julie asks. I nod and she leads me over to a table. On it are two racks of test tubes containing blue liquid.

"Each of these tubes has a slightly different chemical composition," she explains. "We want to see how fast each solution evaporates when left uncovered." Pulling open a drawer, she removes a clipboard with a chart on it. "You'll chart the amount of liquid in each tube," she says, handing the chart to me. She explains how to measure and date the chart, then leaves me to my job.

I wonder why they would need to know this. Then I start coming up with possible reasons. It would affect how they bottle and store the chemical solution. It might help them decide which one to use.

Just as I write in the last measurement, Julie comes to my side. She reads the chart, then smiles. "Excellent. Are you always this precise?"

"I guess so. I like math and science, and you have to be exact with them."

"Absolutely," she agrees. "You'll be good at this."

"I hope so," I say, pleased that I've done well on my first assignment.

My next job is to test some other liquid solutions with litmus paper, which tells where they fall in a range between acid and alkaline. The paper turns a different color depending on the composition of the liquid. Julie gives me another clipboard with another chart on which to record my findings.

As I work, I wonder why Brenna is so upset about all this. I can't wait to get home and tell her that she's been excited over nothing. There isn't anything to object to in the work they do at AVM.

I finish the tests and look over at Julie, who is filling in some charts of her own. She looks up and I catch her eye. "Done?" she asks.

I nod, smiling. This work is interesting and I enjoy doing it. Maybe lab work really is what I'm best suited for. It's so logical and precise—just like me.

"Good job," she says, looking over my chart. "I have another job for you. Come with me." I follow her out and down the hall. We enter another room. This room is entirely different from the last one. For one thing, it's full of caged rodents! One wall is lined with shelves holding tanks of small gray mice, white rats, hamsters, and even rabbits.

"You... you experiment on these animals?" I ask. I try to keep my voice neutral. After all, Brenna warned me about this. Actually seeing the animals in their cages is a bit shocking to me, though.

"When I first began doing medical research, I was pretty freaked out by it, too," Julie says. "But we don't do product testing. This is a veterinary medicine facility. Right now we're working on possible cures for animal diabetes and feline leukemia."

"Do you... kill these animals?" I have to know.

"Sometimes," Julie tells me.

"I'm not sure I could handle that," I admit.

"Don't worry, interns aren't involved in that,"

Julie says. "All you have to do is help feed and water them."

Taking care of animals was exactly what I wanted to get away from. But there isn't too much I can do to hurt them if all I'm doing is feeding them. "OK," I agree.

Julie pulls open a bottom cabinet and takes out a bag of food pellets. "Each tank has small bowls. Just fill them all with the food." She hands me a pair of white padded gloves. "Use these to protect your hands."

I wave them away. "I'm not afraid of animals," I say.

She hands them back to me. "Use them anyway. Some of these animals are sick. The lab doesn't want its employees taking any chances."

Wearing the heavy gloves, I go from tank to tank. The little guys are really cute. There's a tank of longhaired calico hamsters that are so pretty. Another tank has three lop-eared bunnies that are just too adorable. Then I come to a tank of five white rats. People think of rats as being dirty, but these rats are clean and full of personality. Their pink noses twitch and they look up at me with their trusting eyes, eager for their food.

I forget all about why these animals are here and just enjoy feeding them, picking them up and stroking their fur. One rat with a slightly bent whisker is especially friendly. He sniffs my glove and then curls up as if he's getting ready to sleep in my palm. Gently, I return him to his tank.

Julie comes back after about fifteen minutes. "How are you doing?" she asks.

"Good," I reply.

● ● ● ● ●

When my shift at the lab is over, I unlock my bike and ride out to the street. As I near Dr. Mac's Place, I spot Brenna, David, and Maggie walking to mask-making class. I don't want them to be mad at me. I need to fix yesterday's fight. I can't go through everything I have to face—Mittens, working at the lab—without my friends. Pedaling fast, I catch up to them. "Hey, guys!" I call out. "Wait."

"I thought you were at the lab," Brenna says coldly as I brake beside them.

I ignore her tone. I'm not in the mood to fight. "I just finished," I tell her.

"Well, how was it?" Maggie asks.

"The people were all very nice to me," I say.

"Forget the people!" Brenna says passionately. "What about the animals? It's as though they're in jail there—and on death row! Only they aren't guilty of doing anything wrong. Don't you think they have rights, too?"

"Of course animals have rights," I agree.

"Then how can you be a part of what goes on there?" Brenna asks, shaking her head forlornly.

"It's a medical research lab," I say, repeating what Dr. Mac told us the other day. "The research there is done to find new cures and treatments for sick animals. That's a good thing."

"There's a laugh!" Brenna chimes in. "Killing animals to save them. Figure the logic of that!"

"Oh, give Sunita a break!" Maggie says. "Let her make up her own mind on the subject. Besides, didn't Gran say that those labs are needed to make new medicines for animals?"

"Yes, she said that," Brenna replies. "And I think there has to be another way to do it without killing poor defenseless animals."

"Why were you at school so late?" I ask, desperate to change the subject.

"We stayed to play basketball in the gym.

Now we're going to the mask-making class,"
David says. "Are you coming?"

"Well, it depends," I say. "Do you know how
Mittens is doing?"

"Slightly better," Maggie says. "I called Gran
to tell her we'd be at school till late and I asked
about Mittens. She told me Mittens' fever is a
hundred and two."

I nod. "Then I'll come to class and see her
after."

The walk to Michaela's house is quiet and
uncomfortable. Brenna acts icy and clearly mad
at me. Maggie is just quiet and thoughtful. David
tries to keep up the conversation, but it isn't easy
to act normal when it's only he and I talking.

At class we continue to work on the wire
framework for our masks. Several times I look
up and catch Michaela watching me. When our
eyes meet, she doesn't seem embarrassed. "Nice
work," she simply says.

I ask Michaela for permission to call home.
My mother had wanted me to check in when I
got to the mask-making class. Michaela directs
me to the wall phone in the kitchen. As I leave
my message on the answering machine at home,

I have the oddest feeling of being watched. I look over at Michaela, but she's helping David with his wire work. Then I glance at the picture window in the kitchen and see the matted black cat sitting on the outside windowsill, staring in—staring directly at me.

Is it Michaela's cat? I look around to ask her, but she's not there.

I hurry to the kitchen door. I'm determined now to catch that cat. I want to cut all those matted clumps out of its fur—to brush it, to feed it, to de-skunk it. I'd make sure to be careful and not do anything to endanger this creature. It would be my final animal rescue.

I open the back door and look out at the cat. It peers at me with those amazing green eyes. I take a step outside the door. In a flash, it jumps off the sill and darts into the woods behind Michaela's house. I walk a few more steps into the yard, searching. The cat has, once again, disappeared.

Chapter Eight

. . . .

On Wednesday I leave the house early so I can check on Mittens. When I arrive, Dr. Mac is sitting in the waiting room doing paperwork. She looks up at me and smiles softly, but her eyes are worried. "Her fever's gone back to a hundred and four," she tells me before I even ask.

"Why aren't the antibiotics working?" I ask.

"You know how it is, Sunita," Dr. Mac replies. "You can't always predict how an animal will react to medication. Peritonitis is a serious infection. I've changed her antibiotic to one that's stronger. We may have to take her back to surgery and put in a drain. A drain is a little rubber tube inserted into the abdomen that allows infected fluid to drain out of the abdomen and sterile fluids, or even antibiotics, to be flushed in. The drain can be removed when the infection is under control."

"Can I see her?" I ask.

"Sure," Dr. Mac agrees. Mittens' cage is by the window. That's nice of Dr. Mac to give her sunshine and a view. She's sleeping all curled into a ball.

When I unlatch the cage, Mittens raises her head a little and looks up at me miserably. I wonder if she blames me. Could she possibly think I hurt her on purpose?

She extends one of her paws, and I cover it with my hand. She licks my hand with her small, dry tongue. At least she doesn't hate me.

Mittens tries to meow but it comes out like a pathetic croak. "I'm so sorry," I whisper.

Maggie comes into the room. "The new medicine will help," she says.

"I hope so," I say.

She comes to my side and pets Mittens. "Gran will do everything she can," Maggie says.

I blink back tears and nod.

In science today, I'm scolded for not knowing the lab instructions the teacher has just given. My math teacher stops me after class to ask if I'm all right. "You were a million miles away," she says. The worst of it comes in gym, when I'm hit in the shoulder with the basketball because I'm standing on the court not paying one bit of attention.

In English our teacher shows us a video of the play *Les Misérables*. In the beginning of that play, a man goes to jail for stealing a loaf of bread for his starving family. "Is it all right to break a rule if you have a good reason?" my teacher asks us after we've viewed the first act of the play.

I recall Brenna's words about animal rights. I raise my hand and say, "Maybe it could be all right to break a rule if you did it because someone's rights were being violated. What if you freed a person who was being held captive unjustly?"

The teacher asks my classmates what they think. Everyone agrees that freeing an unjustly captured person would be the right thing to do.

"Who determines what 'unjust' means?" my teacher asks.

Hmmm. Brenna thinks it's unjust to do

medical testing on animals. But Dr. Mac thinks it's sad but necessary—a few animals die so that lots more can live. I raise my hand. "I guess it can mean different things to different people," I say. But what does it mean to me?

· · · · ·

School's finally out, and I get on my bike to go over to AVM. At the lab, Julie smiles when I arrive. "You can start by giving all the rodents fresh water and food," she says. "Then I'll show you where we keep the cats and the monkeys. You can start caring for them, too."

She hands me a white lab jacket. I feel sort of cool in it, like a real scientist. Even though washing and refilling water bottles isn't exactly hard-core science, I enjoy it because the animals are so cute.

In the tank, three white rats sleep huddled together and two scurry around. One of them— my little pal with the bent whisker—comes right over and stretches up, as if he wants to say hi. I push the lid aside and lift him out. As he sniffs my gloved hand, his nose twitches. "Hi, cutie," I say softly. "I don't have any food for you now, just water, but I'll come back with food."

He sniffs the air and looks around, as if wondering where I'll be getting this food. His little eyes sparkle alertly.

John, a researcher I met yesterday, walks by. "Don't get too attached to those guys," he says.

"Why not?" I ask. "Are they being...killed?"

He nods. "They've been genetically altered to be diabetic. Two have been given an experimental drug and two haven't. We'll put them all down, then dissect them to compare how the drug has affected their internal organs. If we get the results we expect, we'll conduct the experiment on a larger population of rats to double-check."

John grabs a stack of petri dishes and leaves. The little guy in my hand hasn't understood a word of this. He rests his paw on my finger and looks up at me. He trusts me so much—and he shouldn't. He doesn't know that I'm standing here, learning that he's about to be killed, and I'm not doing anything to stop it. I feel so guilty. It's horrible!

I remember our discussion in English class today. Would it be fair to say that this little rat is an unjustly captured creature?

• • • • •

After finishing at AVM, I grab my bike and ride to Michaela's barn. It's cold, so I make myself small and tight inside my jacket. The wind blows my hair all around my face. Tree branches whip into one another and throw long shadows. There's something spooky about October, even without Halloween being at the end of it. Maybe that's why they put a scary holiday in October in the first place.

It's almost dark. I think of stories I've heard, about how people once thought witches actually turned into black cats. What if that cat really was the woman who moved in down the street? I smile at the silly idea. It would be kind of cool, though—to be able to walk around town as a cat, then hop on a broomstick and fly.

Pretty soon I see lights from Michaela's windows. We're having our third mask-making session today. I haven't decided yet what kind of mask I want to make. I'm almost to Michaela's door when a black streak races in front of me. I hit my brakes, hard. It's the stray. I try to see where it's running to, but it's too dark and shadowy.

"That's twice!" David says, coming up from behind me with Maggie and Brenna.

For a second I look at Brenna, but she turns away coldly. Maggie waves.

"You've been crossed by a black cat two times," David reminds me, sounding as if this is a big deal. "How's your luck been?"

"Not great," I admit.

It is pretty weird how my luck has gotten so bad since the black cat first crossed my path. Now what does this second crossing mean—is more bad luck coming my way? What if a second crossing reverses the luck, making it good?

This can't possibly be me thinking this!

The other kids we know from school are already in Michaela's big main room. Michaela—dressed today in loose black pants and an oversized purple velour shirt—is showing them something. As we sit at the table, I see what she has. It's another mask of the black stray.

This one is larger and much more beautiful than the one on the wall. Instead of being covered in fur, this mask has been fired with a black glaze. Michaela has created the cat's wild, swirling fur by twisting and molding the clay into fine points. The eyes are green and luminous.

"Hello," Michaela greets us. "I was just explaining that recently a fabulous animal, an amazing cat, has come into my life. It's such a magical creature, and it intrigues me. You will see that I've already done one mask of it there on the wall." She nods toward the one I spotted on Monday.

"Told you," I whisper to my friends.

"I've decided I'm not pleased with that smaller mask," she goes on. "The fur is all wrong. It makes it silly, like a stuffed toy. So I'm having a second try at it. This is clay, which I like better for this particular subject because it has an earthiness that befits this cat. If any of you continue to work on masks after this workshop, I urge you to think about what medium is best for your subject, as it really is an important decision."

She gathers up some burlap from the floor at her feet and drapes it over her creation. We sort through the pile of wire mask frames Michaela has placed on the table. Michaela goes to her kitchen and begins mixing a powder with water. For a moment I can picture her as a witch working on a potion.

She looks up sharply. "Papier-mâché," she explains, as if she's heard my thoughts. "Some of you will be ready for it today."

"You're blushing," Maggie whispers to me. "What's going on?"

I realize I'm embarrassed because I feel Michaela has caught me thinking she's a witch! Of course that's totally goofy.

"Nothing's going on," I answer Maggie. "It's just warm in here."

Brenna glances over at us. When I look back at her, she quickly looks down at her wire work.

As I work, I think about Michaela and the black cat. It must be her pet. But if she loves it so much, why would she let it get so ragged and matted? I feel angry at her for neglecting her pet. I decide to ask Michaela why she doesn't take better care of it.

When the other kids start packing up to leave, I dawdle until they're all gone. The idea of confronting Michaela makes me jittery, but I have to say something to her about how she's neglecting that cat or I'll never feel right about myself.

I glance around, looking for Michaela. She's gone. Maybe she's gone outside.

When I push open the back door to look for her, something seems to push back. I force the door open and am blown by a strong gust. A light over the door makes a pool of yellow and casts the rest of the yard in gray shadow.

Meow.

I look toward the sound and see Michaela several yards away—on all fours, making meowing cat sounds! I step closer, wondering what she's doing. She keeps crawling and meowing among the bushes. The trees behind her rustle in the wind. Michaela crawls in so far that I can't see her.

Then something moves. It's the black stray running from the bushes back toward the house. Michaela has turned into the stray! I know that's insane—but it's what my eyes are telling me!

Chapter Nine

• • • • • • • • • • • •

The shrubbery moves again, and Michaela emerges. She stands, and I feel my face flushing with embarrassment. I'm glad she can't see me. How could I have thought even for a second that she had turned into a cat? What's happening to me?

She walks slowly toward me. "Can you catch that cat?" she asks me softly.

The black cat pauses between us. It looks from side to side, realizing that we're closing in on it.

"Here, kitty, kitty," I coax.

While it's looking at me, Michaela moves toward it from behind, closer and closer. But the cat turns, sees her, and bolts off into the woods. Michaela and I exchange a look of defeat and frustration. If it's her cat, wouldn't it come right to her?

"That cat's coat is in terrible condition," I say.

"I know," she says, tossing her wild hair back over her shoulder. "I've been trying to catch it for weeks. I leave food for it every night." She nods toward a plate of cat food and a bowl of water over by the corner of her house.

I was wrong about her. This isn't her cat and she hasn't been mistreating it at all. Instead, she's been trying to help it. I'm so glad I didn't get a chance to confront her. I would have felt like an idiot when I discovered the truth.

"This cat isn't the least bit friendly. It just eats and runs," she continues as she goes back inside the house. "It's definitely on its own. I'd like to bring it in on Halloween. I've heard that people should keep their cats in on that night."

"I've heard the same thing," I say as I follow her. "If we could catch it, I could cut those clumps from its fur. Otherwise the clumps will spread over its whole body."

She sits on a chair in the kitchen and gestures for me to sit, too. "I was planning to brush her," she says. "It would probably be difficult, though."

I sit beside her. "I've done it before at the clinic," I say.

"That place up the road?" she asks.

"Yes." I tell her about Dr. Mac's Place and how my friends and I volunteer there. "Well, I used to volunteer there," I correct myself. "I'm not sure I will anymore." I tell her how I've started the lab internship at AVM. "And now Brenna's disappointed and angry with me. She thinks it's unethical of me to work in a place with lab animals."

"You're having a shift," Michaela says.

I look up, curious. "What do you mean?"

She speaks slowly, as though she wants to choose her words carefully. "Sometimes in life, people go through a period of time when they move from one way of being to a different way," she explains. "It's a time when you feel a lot of confusion and you don't know who you are. You might not even recognize the feelings you have and words you say as being your own."

"That is exactly what I've been feeling!" I say excitedly. "Why is this happening?"

"Because you're ready for it to happen."

"How will I change?"

Michaela laughs lightly. "I have absolutely no idea. It's different for everyone. The change might take a long time. You have to pay attention."

"Attention to what?" I ask.

"To what you're feeling, to the places where life is directing you. You have to find your inner spirit. That's what I've tried to capture in that cat mask—the animal's bold, wild inner spirit. It isn't easy since it won't even sit still for me. Sometimes I have to be very quiet and just watch it."

"I wonder what my mask would look like if it showed who I really am inside," I say.

"Fierce. Passionate," Michaela replies without hesitating.

Her description surprises me. I'm shy and sensible. At least, that's how I've always been. What does she see in me that I can't see?

"That doesn't seem true to you, does it?" Michaela says.

"No," I say. "I don't think anyone really sees me that way."

"You may be the one who doesn't see yourself like that," she says. "Pay attention. I have a hunch that you'll view things differently soon."

How does she know these things? Could she really be a witch?

Again she answers my unasked question, at least the first one. "I know, because I've had shifts in my life, several times." She snaps her fingers. "I know why I thought we'd met!" she says. "You stopped your bike outside my house last weekend. I saw you from my bedroom window."

"I have to tell you this," I say, "because now it seems so ridiculous. My friends had the idea that you're a witch. They almost had me believing it when you went into the bushes and the cat ran out. I actually was starting to wonder if you had taken the form of that stray cat! I hope you're not offended."

"Offended? No! I'm delighted," she says, smiling. "People have been claiming that witch women turned into cats ever since the time of the Greeks. I wish I could turn into a cat. It would be like being part of a great tradition."

"You don't mind that we thought you were a witch?" I ask.

"Witches get a bad rep," she replies "You know, historically, witches were simply female figures with power, followers of ancient goddesses of the earliest religions. As the world's religions became more male-dominated, men turned these powerful females into evil spirits. Then they began picking on women who were healers and accusing them of being evil figures. Cats are so mysterious, they also became associated with the witches."

I want to hear more about the history of witches, but my mother has come into Michaela's house and is calling. "Hello? Anyone here? Sunita?" I forgot she was planning to stop by tonight to meet Michaela. Mom always wants to meet my teachers.

Michaela gets up. "Time to go."

Mom is impressed with Michaela and her masks. They talk about her art a few minutes and then we leave. "She's a very talented woman," my mother says as we drive home.

"Nice, too," I add. It's funny to think that less than a half hour earlier, I was ready to tell her off for the way she treats her cat.

It's strange how often you find out you don't have the whole story, and when you get the complete picture, it changes the way you think. "Mom?" I ask. "Do you ever wonder whether or not you've done the right thing?"

She glances at me and laughs lightly. "All the time. Why do you ask?"

"I'm just wondering. What do you do about it?"

"I try to learn as much as possible. It helps to know all the facts. Then I do the best I can. Is something on your mind?"

My mind is so full of questions that I don't know where to begin. "No," I say, "nothing in particular."

* * * * *

After supper, I call Dr. Mac to find out if Mittens is doing any better. She says things about elevated levels in Mittens' blood that I don't understand. I know it isn't good, though.

I do my homework and try to read the novel we've been assigned. The book is OK, but my mind isn't on it. I realize I'm very tired so I wash up, change into my pajamas, and crawl into bed.

Exhausted as I am, I fall right asleep. I keep having weird dreams, though, and after a while I can't sleep. The readout on my clock says it's two-thirteen in the morning.

In my dreams, the white rat with the bent

whisker was speaking to me, but I don't know what he was saying. Soon, he's going to be killed. At least his death might help other animals. What if AVM could discover a better antibiotic for peritonitis? If a few rats died so my cat could live, wouldn't it be worth it? Wouldn't that be "just"? I don't know.

I replay the conversation I had with Michaela. "You're having a shift," she said. That feels right to me. Something inside me is changing. I can feel it. That's all I know, though. I have no idea what will happen next, or how big a change this will turn out to be.

Something is happening, that much is sure. I wish I could look into the future and see who I will turn out to be. I hope it's someone I can respect.

Chapter Ten

. . . .

I'm awake when the sun rises, so I get up and start getting dressed. I've made a decision that I think is a just one.

I ride my bike over to AVM and arrive at about eight o'clock. Julie and John won't be there until nine. That should give me plenty of time.

"You're here early," the receptionist comments when I walk in with my school backpack slung over my shoulder.

"Yeah, I'm early today," I agree. I smile and try to look casual. If I seem nervous, she might suspect that I'm up to something.

I get to the room where we usually work and jiggle the knob. Oh, no! Locked!

One of the custodians is down the hall. I hurry over to him. "Could you let me into the room with the animals?" I ask.

He begins to shake his head, but I take out the ID card Julie gave me. "I'm an intern. I need to feed the animals before school."

"Oh, all right," he says, unclipping the large ring of keys from his belt. "That's very dedicated of you."

"Yeah, well..." I reply. "Someone's got to do it."

I thank him, lock the door behind me, and toss my backpack by the door. The shades are drawn and the room is dark. Most of the animals are still curled up, asleep. Not bothering to turn on a light, I go to the rats' tank. The five white rats are cuddled together, snoozing. I try to lift the tank, but it's way too heavy.

How can I do this? My eyes dart around the lab. There's got to be a way.

I remember my backpack lying by the door. That's it! Grabbing the pack, I unzip it and unload the books, then return to the tank and take off the lid.

My rat friend from the other day is the first to look up at me. I can tell it's the same rat because one whisker is slightly bent. I scoop him up and give him a nuzzle with my nose. Then I set him down inside my pack. He stands up immediately and starts sniffing. He probably smells the lunch that was in there just a moment before. I put his four sleepy pals in the backpack with him and zip it up.

Behind this lab is a supply room with a door that leads to an open, grassy field. The door is locked from the outside but not the inside. As long as I put a book in the doorway to hold the door open, I'll be able to get back in.

Out in the yard I lay the backpack down and unzip it. "There you go," I say to the rats. "You're free. Go!"

I expect them to race out, but instead they stay inside the pack, sniffing. "What's the matter with you guys?" I ask as I lift the pack and gently dump them out. "Get going!"

They just look at me and hang around as though they have no desire to escape. Freeing these animals is the bravest thing I've ever done in my life—and they won't leave!

My friend is the first to travel a little

distance. The others scurry after him. "That's it," I encourage them. "Be free." They travel a little farther, sniffing cautiously as they go.

I am happy. Proud of myself, too. I wish I could have freed all those animals. I wonder if there's still time. I could probably free the mice and maybe the hamster before nine o'clock.

Turning back to the door, I'm suddenly face-to-face with Julie. Her face is tight and serious.

"What do you think you're doing?" she demands.

I stand firm. "It's the right thing to do. Those rats don't deserve to die. The other animals, either."

"Those rats are very sick," Julie says, "and now they're going to die a much more terrible, drawn-out death, thanks to you."

"But..." I begin. "I...I...What will happen to them?"

"Believe me, you don't want to know," she replies. "Their eyesight will begin to fail. They'll become dehydrated and—"

I hold up one hand to stop her. "You're right," I say. "I don't want to know. I didn't think about all that."

"In this kind of work, you can't afford not to think," Julie says. She steps past me, her eyes fixed on something I can't see.

I follow her gaze. One of the white rats is darting in and out of the tall grass. Picking up my pack, I head toward the rat. Julie reaches into her lab coat pocket and pulls out some pellets of food.

It isn't hard to catch the rats. They're so tame, they like people and feel safe around them. Julie catches the first rat almost instantly, as soon as she extends her hand holding the food pellet. Soon we have the other four, too.

We walk back into the lab without speaking and return the rats to their tank.

"Listen, Sunita," Julie says finally, "these animals are not anyone's beloved pets. We didn't kidnap them or buy them in a dark alley from someone who stole them. They were bred to be research animals."

"Even the cats?" I ask.

"Even the cats. These animals are extremely expensive because they're bred to be free of germs and disease. Some cost over a thousand dollars."

I don't know what to say. My head is spinning with all sorts of different thoughts that won't come together into a sensible sentence.

"The research animals that die could help other animals to live," she continues. "That might sound harsh, but those are the realities. I don't feel one bit bad about the work I do here. A lot of people who love and depend on their pets benefit from our work, and, of course, the new medicines improve the lives of the animals themselves."

"But you made those rats sick," I argue. "Don't they suffer because they're sick?"

"We do all we can to ease their suffering, and we don't keep them around for long once they're sick. That's why we were going to euthanize those rats this Friday—so they don't get so ill that they're in real, serious pain."

"Do all the research labs do that?" I ask.

Julie throws her arms out to the side, obviously getting frustrated with me. "They're supposed to!" she says. "Sunita, there are guidelines and laws for doing research with living creatures. Everything has to be approved before an experiment can even begin."

I look down at the white rats and at the other rodents. They all look so innocent, so in need of love and a home.

"I hear what you're saying, and what I did was wrong. Sorry," I apologize. "I'm glad you're able to do this work to help animals. But I can't. It's too hard for me to work with the animals knowing that they're going to be killed."

Julie looks at me closely and nods. She doesn't seem mad anymore. "I love this work so much, I forget sometimes that not everyone feels the same way," she says. "It could be that research work involving animals just isn't for you."

I collect my books and stick them in the backpack. "I probably won't be coming back," I say.

"All right," Julie agrees. "If that's how you feel, it's probably for the best."

I leave AVM quickly and bike to school. Homeroom is letting out just as I arrive. "Three lates and you'll have a detention," my homeroom teacher reminds me. "This is your second one. It's not like you, Sunita."

"No, it's not. I'm sorry," is all I can think of to say. It's not like me at all—yet somehow I don't care. It's not even like me not to care.

But if I'm not like the old Sunita, who am I like—who replaces the old me?

That's the scary part.

• • • • •

After school I head to Dr. Mac's Place to visit Mittens. Brenna and I see each other in the hallway. She greets me with an angry grunt and keeps walking.

Fine, if that's how you're going to act, I think, even though a big part of me wants us to be friends again.

"Wait a minute, Brenna," I say. "Something happened today, and I want to tell you about it."

She turns to face me. "What?"

"I quit AVM after I let some lab rats go today. I couldn't bear to let them be killed. I set them free."

A smile slowly forms on her face. "You did? Awesome! I can't believe you had the nerve! I'm so proud of you."

I hold up my hand to stop her. "I did it partly because of the things you said to me. But I'm not proud of myself. I didn't have the whole picture.

Those rats were sick, and I didn't realize that by freeing them, I would be causing them a painful death."

"I didn't know those things, either," Brenna admits. Then her face hardens. "But they wouldn't be sick in the first place if labs like AVM didn't exist!"

I take a deep breath. "If labs like AVM didn't exist, Brenna, there'd be no antibiotics to help cats like Mittens."

Brenna's eyes soften. "I'm worried about Mittens, too. But I don't believe that killing animals to save animals makes sense. There just has to be another way."

I sigh as I head in to see Mittens. I guess Brenna and I will never see eye to eye.

Mittens is asleep in her cage. Dr. Mac comes up beside me. "She's improving," she says. "The new antibiotic has taken hold."

I nod, and tears spring to my eyes. They're tears of happiness, tears of relief. But they're also tears of some unexplainable sadness.

• • • • •

At my final mask-making session, I still don't know what kind of mask I want to wear. I leave the wire framework of my mask lying unfinished on the table. I would like some more time to talk to Michaela, but my mother is right on time to pick me up, so there's no chance to talk.

"There's something I have to tell you," I say to Mom as we drive home. "Promise you won't be mad?"

She glances at me with a worried expression on her face. "I don't like the sound of that, Sunita," she says. "What's happened?"

I tell her about how I freed the rats. "Oh, dear," she says. "Sunita, how could you do such a thing? I suppose they fired you."

"No. Julie was pretty nice about it, really. And we got the rats back. But I can't do that kind of work. It's not for me. I quit."

My mother nods, keeping her eyes on the road.

We're both quiet until I ask, "Would you tell Daddy for me?"

"We'll do it together," she says, which makes me feel a little better.

At home we find my father in his study. He looks up with a smile, but his smile fades when he sees our concerned expressions. "What is it?" he asks.

My mother and I sit in chairs by his desk. "Tell him, Sunita," my mother says gently.

By the time I'm near the end of my story, my face is wet with tears. "I only did it because I thought it was right," I say. "But I see now that it wasn't."

My father appears serious, but not that upset. "I'm proud that you followed your conscience," he says. "But before you take a serious action like that, you must have all the facts. You can't just jump in rashly, committing acts with serious consequences without considering all sides of the issue."

"I know that now," I say.

"Sunita has resigned from AVM," my mother tells him.

"Clearly this work is too stressful for her," he says. "So, at least we've learned that much."

"Are you mad?" I ask.

He comes out from behind his desk and strokes my head. "Perhaps a little disappointed. But it's your life. And these are the decisions you alone can make. No, I'm not mad. You're growing up, Sunita."

Chapter Eleven

. . . .

After class the next day, I go to the clinic. "Mittens' fever is back up a bit today," Dr. Mac says as she tweezes a thorn from a puppy's paw. "I just ran some blood tests on her. I'll have to wait until tomorrow morning for the results."

My shoulders sag with disappointment. "I thought she was finally getting better."

"So did I. The tests should tell me what to do next," she says. The dog in her lap squirms. "Hold him steady for me, please," she requests.

I do as she asks. It's as if I never left the clinic.

"Success," Dr. Mac says happily as she holds

up the thorn in her tweezers. She looks at me intently. "How's your internship at AVM coming?" she asks.

"It's over," I say, and I tell her about the white rats and how I had to go chase them down.

"It's hard to know what's right sometimes," she says, swabbing the pup's paw with alcohol.

Dr. Mac always seems so sure of herself. "Isn't it clear to you?" I ask.

"Not always," she admits. "When I was a veterinary intern, I wasn't prepared for the fact that I would have to put some people's pets to sleep. Oh, in my mind I understood that this would happen, but I wasn't prepared for the way I'd feel emotionally. Still...I had to help owners make informed choices about relieving their pets' suffering or continuing on with treatment that had little hope of success."

"I guess that would be a hard choice," I agree.

"Very hard."

Then a frightening thought makes me cold all over. Did Dr. Mac just bring up the subject because she's thinking about Mittens? It's a question I can't bring myself to ask her.

• • • • •

On the night of the Halloween party at the
Ambler Town Center, David comes by my house
to pick me up. He's dressed in his vampire costume. I've used fabric markers to draw a big jack-
o'-lantern on an oversized orange sweatshirt. I'm
not much in the mood for Halloween, but it's
worse sitting around doing nothing.

"Where are Brenna and Maggie?" I ask.

"We're meeting them over at Town Center,"
he says.

I grab my flashlight and we begin walking. Up
the road I see Maggie and Brenna. They're talking
to one of the girls from our mask-making class.
Maggie's dressed in her veterinarian costume,
which is made up of scrubs, a surgical mask, a
stethoscope, and a stuffed dog. Brenna is dressed
as a hippie from the sixties, complete with daisy-
print bell-bottom pants and a band around her
forehead. They haven't noticed us yet.

David and I are just about to turn the corner
when I spot something ahead of us on the road. I
can't see it that well, but I can tell it's an animal.
Its legs are pumping and it can't seem to get up.
"An animal's been hurt!" I yell.

David runs with me, but I get there first.

"Oh, no!" I cry. "It's the black stray!" Blood trickles from its mouth, and its eyes are wide with fear.

Chapter Twelve

· · · · · · · · · · · ·

The black stray lets out a horrible yowl. David kneels down to pick it up. "No!" I shout to stop him. "If the cat has broken bones, scooping it up might cause more damage. And it's frightened— it might scratch or bite you." I remember Dr. Mac telling us how animals go into shock and need to be kept warm. Covering them helps them stay warm and feel calmer. "Cover it with your cape," I tell David. "Wait here. I'll be right back."

Two houses away, a woman is at her door giving candy bars to trick-or-treaters. I rush up to her. "A cat's been hit by a car. Do you have a box I could use?"

The woman reaches under the table by her door and pulls out a medium-sized box that still has some wrapped candy in it. She dumps the candy onto the table and hands me the box. "Wait one second," she says as she digs through a basket sitting by the door and pulls out a pair of leather gardening gloves. "We'll take these, too," she says, handing them to me. "I'm coming with you."

"Thanks so much," I tell her as I lead her back to the cat.

When I get there, Maggie and Brenna have joined David. "How will we get it into the box without lifting it?" David asks.

I tear down one side of the box so that it lies flat on the road. I put on the gardening gloves, carefully lift the cat onto David's cape, and slide it into the box. Then we put the open side back up.

The cat has stopped moving. Fearing the worst, I touch its side, and it meows in a small voice. Good. It's alive.

The woman gives us a lift back to the clinic. I keep the cat covered, resting my hands lightly on the cloth the whole ride. The rise and fall of the cat's breath lets me know it's still alive.

"Good luck," the woman says as we climb out of the car at the clinic. We thank her and hurry inside the front door. Dr. Mac is sitting in the kitchen, reading.

"Oh, dear, what's wrong?" she asks when she sees us rush in.

"A cat's been hit," I say as I place the box on the table. She pulls back David's cape to see the hurt cat. Its eyes are half open. She hurries it into the Herriot Room with the four of us alongside her.

Leaving the cat in the box, she places it on the examining table. "Do you know who owns this cat?"

"I don't think anyone owns it," I say. "But Michaela—the woman who gives the mask-making classes—has been feeding it."

Dr. Mac asks me to hold the cat steady while she looks at its injuries.

"It's good that you moved it so carefully," Dr. Mac comments as she feels the cat's body gently but firmly. Then Dr. Mac squeezes the cat's rear toes. The cat doesn't seem to have any feeling, even though Dr. Mac is now pinching them very hard. "But I'm not sure we can save it," Dr. Mac tells us. "I think this cat may have a broken back. I'll X-ray it to be sure."

Dr. Mac takes the cat into the X-ray room. A few minutes later she comes in to show us the X-rays. She places them on a lighted view box.

"It's a broken back all right," says Dr. Mac as she points out the breaks.

"What can we do to help the cat?" I ask.

Dr. Mac sighs. "This is one of those difficult decisions vets hate to make. In my opinion, the kindest thing would be to give it a painkiller and put it to sleep."

"Isn't there anything we can do?" Maggie asks.

"There are some procedures I could try, but I really believe they would be pointless, and we'd be prolonging this animal's suffering."

I remember Dr. Mac telling me how hard this part of her job is for her.

"I guess that's what we have to do, then," Brenna says sadly. The rest of us nod.

"You kids can go. I'll take care of this," Dr. Mac tells us.

We walk out of the room together. At the reception desk, I call Michaela. I get her answering machine. "I just thought you might want to know that the black stray has been hit by a car. Dr. Mac can't help it, so she's going to put it to sleep." As I say the last words, my voice cracks.

"I'm going to go home," David says. Obviously, he's lost the Halloween spirit. "See you all in the morning."

Brenna, Maggie, and I stand in the front lobby just looking at one another. Brenna speaks first. "I just don't know how Dr. Mac does it."

"Gran hates putting down animals," Maggie says.

"It's hard on her," I say. "It isn't easy to know what's right when it comes to things like this."

"Listen, Sunita," Brenna says. "I've been pretty hard on you. Maybe I didn't really think about everything that's involved when you work with animals. I mean, it's more complicated than I realized. And I know you really do care about animals. I'm sorry about the way I've been acting."

"It's all right," I say. "I've been confused by it all, too. So we're friends again?"

"Definitely," Brenna replies.

Just at that moment, Michaela rushes in. Maggie and Brenna stare at her, wide-eyed. She's dressed as a witch with a pointed hat and a cloak. She's even got a witch's broom in her hand.

I smile, thinking of how freaked out my

friends must be by the sight of her. "Hey, kids," she greets them.

"Hi," they say.

"I got your message, Sunita," she says. "I thought you might want some company. But I see you have some." She shivers and draws her witch cloak around herself more closely. "It's getting cold out there," she comments.

"I could make us some hot cocoa or tea," Maggie offers.

"Tea would be lovely," Michaela replies.

"I'll help," says Brenna as she and Maggie head toward the kitchen.

Michaela and I sit together quietly in the lobby for a few minutes. "How are you doing with your lab work?" she asks after a while.

"I quit," I told her. "I couldn't take it."

Michaela nods. "You didn't like it?"

The question surprises me because—strange as it seems—I did like it. "Some things about it, yes. I think it's interesting the way the researchers make an educated guess about what might work and then go about testing their idea."

"I think so, too. I studied chemistry in college," she says.

"You did? Not art?" I ask.

"I wanted to be a biochemist. I liked the work, but I discovered I loved art. It was one of my shifts. I still use chemistry, though. Thanks to what I learned about chemistry, I can make some unusual dyes and paints to use in my art."

"I never would have thought those things were connected," I say.

Michaela looks at me. "Don't worry, Sunita, you'll find your way. There's a lot to you, and it isn't always easy for a complex person to find her way. Eventually your path will become clear. I'm sure of it."

Maggie and Brenna return with cups of tea on a tray. The four of us sit and drink it. No one says much. I think we're all too sad about the black stray to talk.

"You all seem so at home here," Michaela comments as she rises to leave.

"This is Maggie's home," Brenna comments.

"Yes, but you and Sunita also seem to fit right in," Michaela says.

I realize she's right. Dr. Mac's Place has been like a second home to me. I wonder—do I still belong here?

Chapter Thirteen

• • • • • • • • • • • •

The next morning, Dr. Mac steps out of the Herriot Room with Mittens in her arms. "Finally! She's doing beautifully!" she announces, handing Mittens to me.

I nuzzle her. Mittens licks my nose. Her eyes are bright again, just the way I remember.

"You did well with that stray last night," Dr. Mac says to me. "You treated her for shock, moved her as gently as possible, and got her here quickly. Thanks to you, Sunita, that cat spent her last moments on earth sedated and reasonably pain free. That was much better than dying in agony on the side of the road."

I guess I did know what to do.

"Brenna told me you've quit AVM. Does this mean you'll give us more of your time? Will you come back and work with us?"

"Do you really think I should?" I ask.

"I know you've been having doubts lately about your ability to work with animals. So I just want to tell you that I think you'd make a wonderful veterinarian. You have that unique combination—a deep compassion for animals and a good head for science. You've got what it takes, Sunita." She smiles and gets up, just as a woman walks in carrying a big iguana in a cage.

Maggie comes into the reception area holding a box. "Michaela dropped this off for you this morning," she says, handing it to me.

I open the box. Inside is an incredible clay mask Michaela has made of a tiger. Its fur is painted bright gold, with shiny black stripes on top. Its almond-shaped eyes are rimmed with black. There is a note in the box. It reads: *Your fierce passion for animals enabled you to help the black cat. I'm sure she understood and appreciated your kindness. There are many kinds of help. Love, Michaela. P.S. I was thinking about you and a picture of a tiger came to my mind. I made this mask in the* hope *that when you look at it, you will be reminded of how at least one friend sees you.*

I get the pre-crying nose tingle. But I'm not sad, just moved by the gift and Michaela's words. *There are many kinds of help.* I picture the animals over at AVM Labs. They need help, too, even if it is only helping them have comfortable last days. I wonder if Julie will let me work there again. Perhaps I could work here and at the lab, on alternating days.

I decide to call Julie this afternoon and ask her.

Mittens climbs onto my shoulder, purring in my ear. I look down at the tiger mask. It's something I'll always treasure and keep near me—a reminder of the inner spirit I want to grow strong inside me.

A Witch's Best Friend

By J.J. MACKENZIE, D.V.M.

Wild World News—Halloween is a time to try on a spooky new persona—a ghost or goblin, a monster or witch...and, of course, a witch's famous best friend: the black cat. Cats have appeared in myths and legends about witchcraft dating all the way back to the ancient Greeks.

One Greek myth told of a woman named Galenthias who was turned into a cat and then became a priestess of Hecate, the patron goddess of witchcraft. This myth led the way for hundreds of other folktales and stories about women turning into cats. Usually these cat-women were assumed to have magical powers. The black cat is most often associated with witches, but cats of every stripe and spot qualify as a witch's "familiar."

Going on a Witch Hunt for Cats. Back in seventh-century England, causing storms and other disturbances through witchcraft was a crime punishable by death. Sailors began keeping cats on board ships in order to win favor with witches, whom they believed caused storms. The cats' *real* benefit to sailors was much more practical—they ate any mice or rats that had snuck into the ships' food stores!

The cat eventually lost its charm, though. By the twelfth century, people thought cats could do black magic, just as they thought the witches could, and they began killing cats in large numbers. The rapid spread of the bubonic plague—a deadly disease that killed millions during the Middle Ages—came about partly because so many cats were killed. These cats would ordinarily have been killing rodents, which often spread the contagious disease. Without the cats to keep the mouse and rat population down, the rodents roamed from home to home, bringing bubonic plague with them.

CATS HELPED STOP THE SPREAD OF BUBONIC PLAGUE

The witch hunt came to America in the 1600s. Many innocent women were accused of being witches. These women were burned at the stake for their supposed crimes. Not only were the women killed, but their cats were also put into baskets and burned along with them, because people believed the cats had evil powers, too.

Stopping Superstition. Through the years, people have slowly become less superstitious. For the most part, the witch and her cat have become fun figures that remind us of past folklore. Still, cats today are at risk around Halloween. Believe it or not, there are people who use Halloween as an excuse to hunt or kidnap cats, much as people did in the old days, when belief in witches was common. Many shelters and humane societies refuse to adopt cats out during October, just to make sure the cats aren't being adopted by someone who intends to harm them. If you own a cat, it's best to keep your pet inside at night during the last week or two of October.

KEEP CATS INDOORS THE LAST TWO WEEKS OF OCTOBER

Your cat's natural curiosity means you need to help her stay safe indoors, too. Make sure your jack-o'-lantern is out of your cat's reach so she won't be tempted to play with the flame inside. Consider decorating the outside of your house with pumpkins instead of having lit jack-o'-lanterns inside.

In addition, keep your cat in an inner room on Halloween night. (Remember to supply a dish of water and a litter box.) That way she won't dart outside as you give goodies to trick-or-treaters!

Tips for keeping all pets safe on Halloween

• Don't feed trick-or-treat candies to pets. Chocolate is poisonous to a lot of animals. The foil and cellophane candy wrappers can also be hazardous if your pet swallows them.

• Keep your pet at home when you go trick-or-treating. Crowds and costumes can be scary for animals.

• Don't dress your cat, dog, or any other pet in a costume if it resists it. Forcing your pet into a costume can put a lot of stress on the animal.

• If you do dress up your pet, make sure the costume lets the animal move easily and see clearly. Keep your pet in the costume only long enough to snap a few pictures.

Turn the page to read a sample of the next book
in the Vet Volunteers series...

End of the Race

Chapter One

• • • • • • • • • • • •

Hi, Maggie! Are you working at the clinic this afternoon? I'll walk with you." Sunita taps my shoulder as the school bus pushes us through the first heavy snowstorm of the new year.

I turn to her in the seat behind me. She's wearing a purple parka, her favorite color. "Sure," I say.

When the bus grinds to a halt, we jump off and tromp through the sparkly drifts to Dr. Mac's Place, my grandmother's veterinary clinic, where Sunita and I volunteer along with some of our friends. I live with Gran—or Dr. Mac, as everyone else calls her—in the house attached to the clinic. It's great getting to care for animals every day.

"How come you're taking the late bus?" asks Sunita. "Were you studying at the library? I didn't see you there."

"Me, at the library? You must be kidding." Even though I'm doing better in school since my science teacher, Mr. Carlson, helped me map out a study plan last year, the library is still the last place you'll find me. "I just finished basketball practice. Sunita, you should have seen it—Darla almost breathed fire when Coach Williams put me in as center. She even elbowed me when the coach wasn't looking and said I was too short to play that position. Can you believe that? I've always played center." I form a snowball, leap up, and hurl it over a branch. "Jump shot!"

"Center was Darla's regular position at her old school, right?" Sunita is more into books than basketball, but even she's heard that Darla Stone, a new girl at Ambler Middle School, considers herself the star player. I nod yes. "Proceed with caution," Sunita warns.

"Guess so," I agree. Sunita wouldn't steer me wrong. She always has the right answer.

"Who are the new patients at the clinic?"

Sunita asks. "I missed two whole weeks because of winter break."

"Ugh, don't remind me that Christmas vacation's already over." I make a face. "Let's see, there are some dogs and kittens still boarding. Gran dewormed the kittens today. They're sooo cute."

"Kitties! How many?" Sunita's a cat person. Calico, Siamese, domestic shorthair, bring them on!

"Four," I reply. "There's also a guinea pig named Podge. He has slobbers."

"Sounds awful. What's that?" asks Sunita. She tears open a bag of pretzels and offers me one.

I grab one in my gloved hand and toss it in the air. "Basket!" I catch it in my mouth, along with a bunch of snowflakes. "Slobbers is a condition where the guinea pig can't close his mouth because his teeth have grown too long. I hate to think of Podge not being able to eat properly, or even to shut his mouth."

"Can Dr. Mac trim his teeth?" Sunita asks.

"Yeah. She's scheduled to do surgery on Podge this Saturday." Only two more school days until I get to spend the day helping Gran with surgery, playing with kittens, and walking the boarder dogs. Hooray!

Sunita wraps her scarf tighter. "It sounds like a full house. Are David and Brenna around?" Our friends David Hutchinson and Brenna Lake have been volunteering at Dr. Mac's Place ever since we needed extra help shutting down an illegal puppy mill last year.

"David's around, but Brenna's family is taking an extra week in Costa Rica. They're learning about sea turtle nesting habits." Brenna's parents are wildlife rehabilitators. It's so awesome how her whole family's involved in saving endangered species.

"It would be nice to be in the tropics right about now," Sunita sighs as the snow swirls faster. We reach my front door and tap snow off our boots. Even though I'm still sweaty from practice, I shiver as a blast of wind whistles under my hood. We hurry in and close the door quickly.

"Whew, it's almost as chilly in here as it is outside." Sunita takes her coat off but pulls a sweater from her backpack.

"Gran doesn't like to heat the house when she's in the clinic all day." I flop onto the living room couch and pry off my boots, then hook my ski jacket on a peg in the closet and shiver again. It IS cold in here. My tummy's rumbling.

After basketball practice I could eat a...well, not a horse! I open the fridge. Some yogurt, left-over salad, a bunch of apples. Much too healthy. "Sunita, want some cereal?"

"No thanks, those pretzels filled me up." She opens one of Gran's veterinary magazines to an article on cat grooming.

I pour a bowl of Froot Loops and milk and gulp it down, then rinse my bowl and leave it in the sink. "Let's see if Gran needs help."

Sunita closes the magazine and follows me through the hallway door to the clinic. Friendly barks from the boarding kennels greet us.

"Gran?" I call as we step into the waiting room.

"Hello," replies an unfamiliar, high-pitched voice.

A girl sits at the receptionist desk, filing charts. Her tightly curled black hair is held back by two yellow clips, which match her sweater. The normally messy desktop has been straightened up. All the active charts and phone messages are in neat piles. She's even put the jumble of pens in a Dr. Mac's Place coffee mug!

"Who are you?" I ask. Why is she sitting at the desk, and where is Gran? Sunita's usually the one who straightens up the desk. I wonder how she feels about this.

"I'm Taryn. Taryn Barbosa. Dr. Mac asked me to help out today."

"What for?" Brenna will be back in town soon and David's right across the street. We don't need another assistant.

"Something about her granddaughter coming in late from basketball practice, and she needed someone to fill in." Dimples crease her dark cheeks.

"I'm her granddaughter, Maggie." Oh, great, joining the basketball team is suddenly a trade-off for working at the clinic?

"You look familiar, Taryn," Sunita says. "You go to Elizabeth Blackwell Elementary, don't you? Didn't you come in last year with your sick canary?"

"Yep. And I also came here last year with my sick rabbit. Dr. Mac did a great job with her. But she died this fall. She just got too old." Taryn looks sad about the rabbit but pleased that Sunita remembers her. Suddenly, I remember her, too. Taryn is the fastest runner at Blackwell, our old school. But what does she know about animals?

"Nice to meet you, Taryn," says Sunita, then

she turns to me. "I'm going to check the meds inventory in the storeroom."

"Need any help?" asks Taryn.

"Thanks, but I can handle it," Sunita replies.

Dr. Gabe, Gran's associate vet, steps out of his office. "Hey girls, how was the first day back at school?"

"Ugh," I groan. Sunita shrugs.

"That bad?" His handsome face crinkles into a grin as he pulls on his coat. "Will you tell Dr. Mac I'm off to check on that tired mama cow?"

I nod. "Sure." He helped yesterday with a tricky breech calf birth on a farm near Dr. Mac's Place. "Where's Dr. Mac?" I ask Taryn.

"She's putting the kittens back in their pen. Not only were they chock-full of roundworms, but they needed another flea bath. Yuck." Taryn gets up. "I'll go get her for you."

"That's OK." I start down the hall to help Gran when a loud vehicle rumbles up the drive. I run to the window and pull back the curtains.

An old blue truck pulls in. A woman in a faded woolen jacket jumps out, leading a badly limping dog up the steps. The doorbell jangles.

"Can I help?" Taryn beats me to the door and holds it open.

"Is this the animal clinic?" asks the woman. Her huge green eyes look frightened.

"Yes," I say, glancing at the dog. It's a bony greyhound the color of gingerbread, whimpering and shivering. "Your dog looks cold. You'd better come in, not that it's much warmer in here."

"Thanks." She stamps her snowy boots on the floor mat. "My name's Roselyn."

Gran hurries into the waiting room. "Hi, girls. Sorry, I was tied up on a phone call." Gran rubs her arms. "Brrr...That storm is really chilling everything down quickly, isn't it?"

"Snow's about a foot deep already," Roselyn says.

Gran leans over the greyhound for a better look. "Hello, what's the matter today?"

"Dog's got a bad leg," Roselyn says. She looks uncomfortable.

"I see." Gran spots the crooked bandage around the dog's leg. "Bring her right in." She motions Roselyn into the Dolittle exam room.

I can't help until I disinfect my hands, so I go to the sink and turn on the faucet. The water is cold and stays that way. It won't heat up. How could we be out of hot water? Suddenly, I realize why everyone's so cold. "Gran, the heat is off!"

"Oh, drat, I knew we should have bought a new boiler last year," Gran sighs. "Maggie, could you set out heat lamps for the kittens and the boarders?"

Sunita walks in with the meds order form on a clipboard. "Hi, Dr. Mac. We're running low on some meds."

"Sunita, glad you're here," Gran says. "Could you help Maggie with the heat lamps? Taryn, please call David Hutchinson and the boiler repairman. Sunita, show her where their numbers are on the Rolodex." As she gives orders, Gran removes the bandage and feels gently up and down the greyhound's swollen leg. The dog yelps as Gran probes with her fingers. "How long has she been like this?"

Roselyn shakes her head. "Not sure. The dog's not really mine. Maybe a week?"

Gran frowns. "I need to take some X-rays. You girls hurry with those lamps!"

I'm itching to help with the greyhound, but the lamps come first. The animals, especially the kittens, mustn't get chilled.